W9-ARQ-335

JANE YOLEN'S
Songs of Summer

Selected, Edited, and Introduced by Jane Yolen

Musical Arrangements by Adam Stemple

Illustrations by Cyd Moore

CAROLINE HOUSE/BOYDS MILLS PRESS

Published by Caroline House
Boyds Mills Press, Inc.
A Highlights Company
910 Church Street
Honesdale, Pennsylvania 18431
Printed in Hong Kong

Publisher Cataloging-in-Publication Data
Yolen, Jane.
Jane Yolen's songs of summer / selected, edited, and introduced by Jane Yolen ; musical arrangements by Adam Stemple ; illustrations by Cyd Moore.—1st ed.
[32]p. : col. ill. ; cm.
Summary: Original and traditional songs that describe the joys of summer.
ISBN 1-56397-110-0
1. Summer—Juvenile songs. 2. Children's songs.
[1. Songs.] I. Stemple, Adam. II. Moore, Cyd, ill. III. Title.
782.42—dc20 1993
Library of Congress Catalog Card Number: 92-85034

First edition, 1993
Book designed by Joy Chu
The text of this book is set in 14-point Galliard Roman;
the song lyrics are set in 12-point Galliard Roman;
the display type is Gill Sans Extra Bold with Cochin Italic.
The illustrations are done in colored pencil and watercolors.
Distributed by St. Martin's Press

10 9 8 7 6 5 4 3 2 1

To the irrepressible Betsy Pucci —JY & AS

To Denny —CM

Contents

Unite and Unite

In the little fishing village of Padstow, England, a strange and wonderful procession occurs every May 1, and has for centuries. Surrounded by men of the village, the great Hobby Horse is led by the "teaser." Everyone plays accordions or drums and dances through the streets welcoming the traditional beginning of summer.

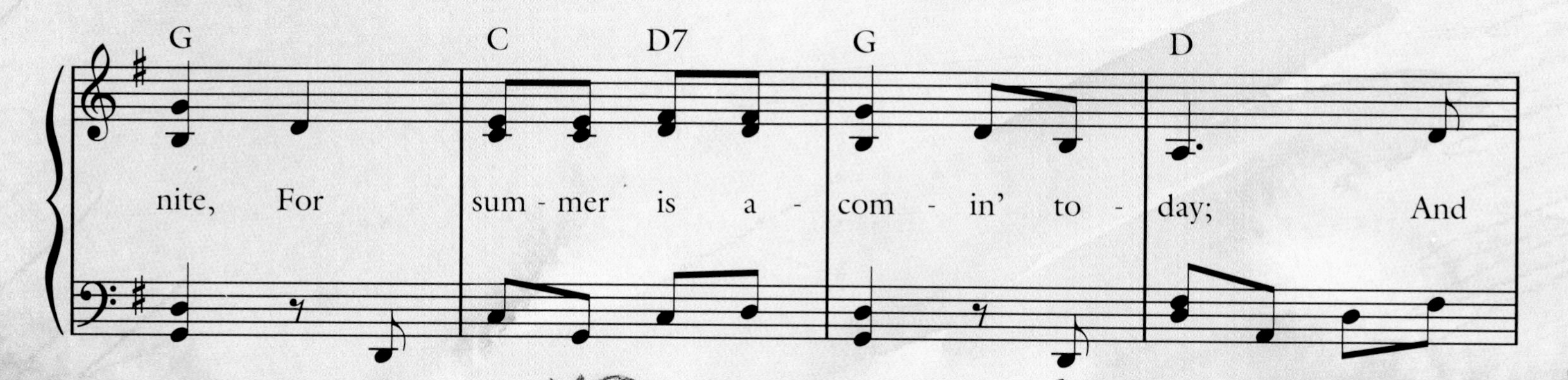

2. The young men of Padstow,
   they might if they would,
   For summer is a-comin' today;
   They might have made a ship
   and gilded it with gold,
   In the merry morning of May!

3. The young girls of Padstow,
   they might if they would,
   For summer is a-comin' today;
   They might have made a garland
   of the white rose and the red,
   In the merry morning of May!

4. O, where are the young men
   that now here would dance?
   For summer is a-comin' today;
   O, some they are in England,
   and some they are in France,
   In the merry morning of May!

Mother Goose Summer

This new song is based on Mother Goose almanac rhymes that predict all the things one might expect during the months of summer.

SWEETLY

Jane Yolen & Adam Stemple

Am G F

1. June brings tu-lips, lil-ies, ro-ses, Fills the chil-dren's heads with po-sies; Mar-ry when June ros-es grow,

2. Hot July brings cooling showers,
   Apricots, and gilly flowers;
   Those who in July are wed,
   Must labor for their daily bread.

   Oh, Mother Goose, oh, Father Gander . . . etc.

3. Then August brings sheaves of corn,
   Then the harvest home is borne;
   Whoever wed in August be,
   Many a change is sure to see.

   Oh, Mother Goose, oh, Father Gander . . . etc.

Oh, What a Summer

Written especially for this book, this song is a catalog of summer seashore fun. The lyricist grew up on the Connecticut shore and experienced all the adventures listed here.

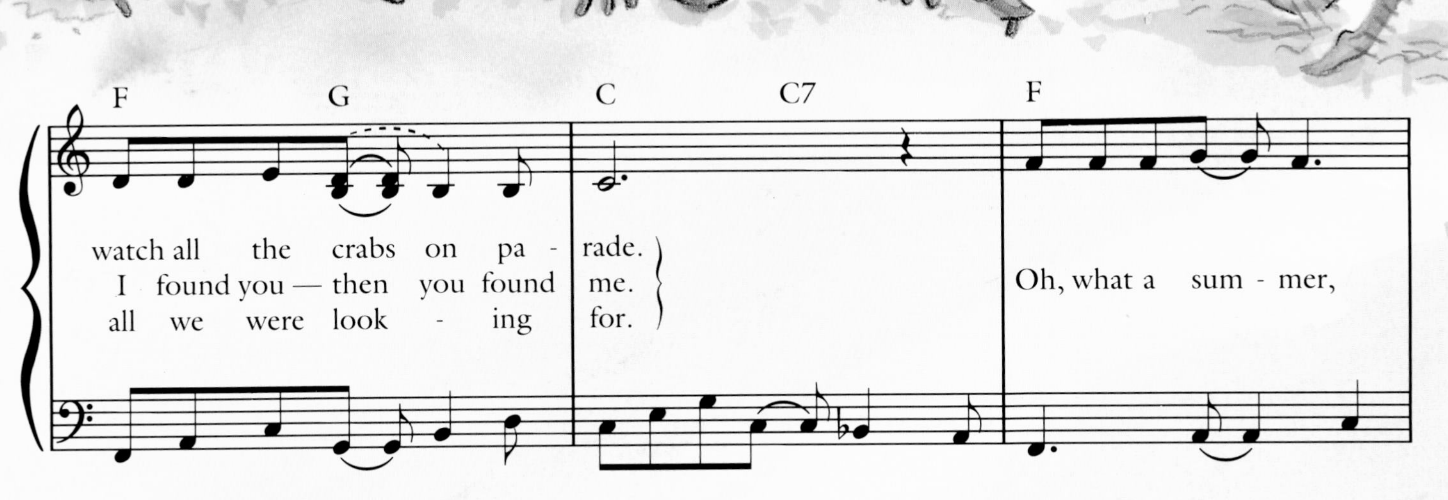
F
G
C
C7
F
watch all the crabs on pa - rade.
I found you — then you found me.
all we were look - ing for.
Oh, what a sum - mer,

C
Am
G
C
C7
oh, what a time,
Oh, what a sea - son of fun.
Your hand in my hand and

F
Fm
C
G7
C
my hand in yours, The sea and the sand and the sun.

Lightly Row

A traditional German children's song, this is equally popular in translation and has been for more than fifty years.

C7
F
Let the wind and waters be
Min - gled with our mel - o - dy;
F
C7
F
C7
F
Sing and float, sing and float,
In our lit - tle boat.

Canoe Round
Written in 1918 by Margaret Embers McGee, this is a popular four-part round.
STEADILY
Margaret Embers McGee
Dm A7 Dm A7 Dm
1. My pad - dle's keen and bright,
2. Dip, dip, and swing her back,
Flash - ing with sil - ver,
A7 Dm A7 Dm
Fol - low the wild goose flight,
Fol - low the wild goose track,
Dip, dip, and swing.

The Road to the Isles

Originally a traditional Scottish tune, published in *The Songs of the Hebrides*, "The Road to the Isles" has taken on Canadian-American lyrics. It is a fine walking song.

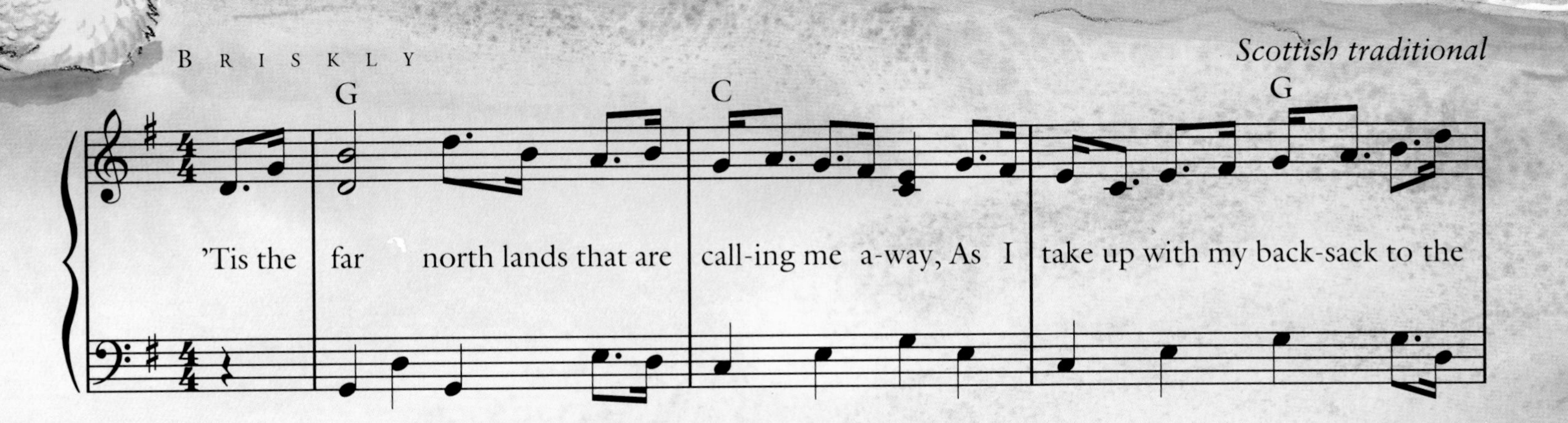

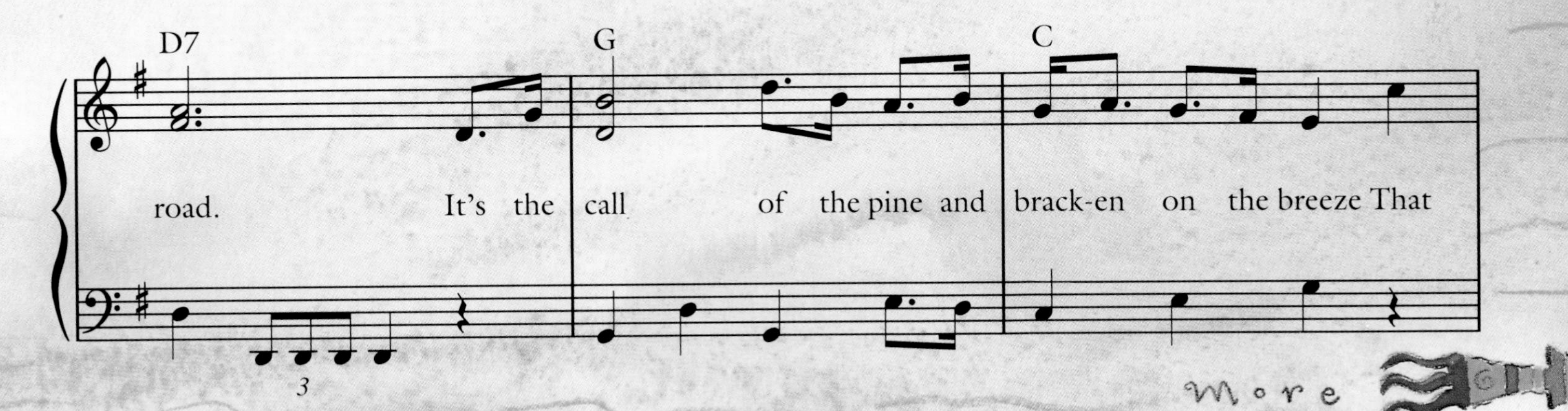

More

G D7 G
calls me to the wa-ter-ways once more. By Lake Dun-can and Clear Wa-ter, To the
C G D7
Bear-skin I will go, Where you see the loon and hear its plain-tive wail. If you're
G C G D7
think-ing in your in-ner heart There's swag-ger in my steps, You've nev-er been a-long the bor-der
3
3

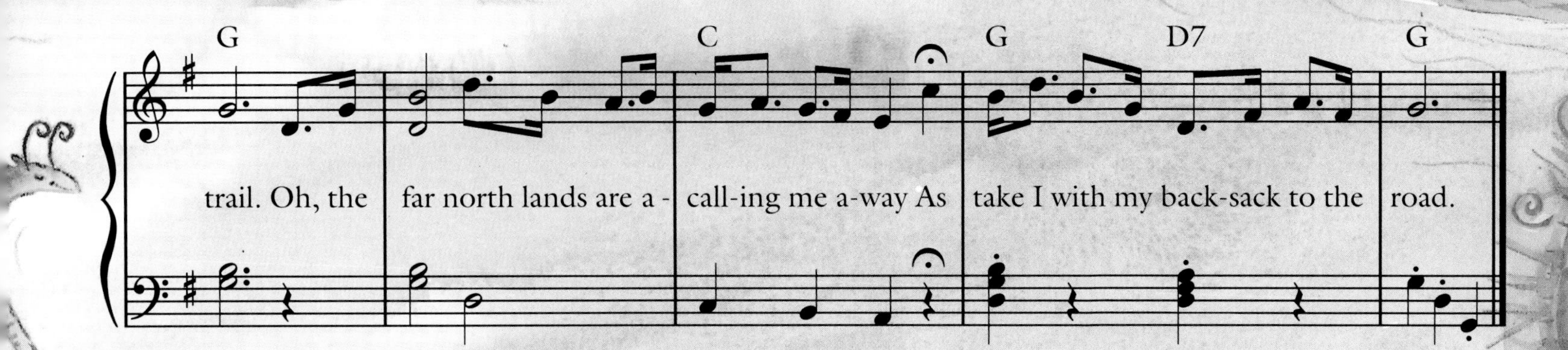

SCOTTISH LYRICS:

A-far croonin' is pullin' me away
As take I wi' my cromack to the road.
The far Cuillins are puttin' love on me
As step I with the sunlight for my load.

Sure by Tummel and Loch Rannoch and Lochaber I will go
By heather tracks wi' heaven in their wiles;
If it's thinkin' in your inner heart the braggart's in my step
You've never smelled the tangle o' the Isles.

Oh, the far Cuillins are puttin' love on me
As step I wi' my cromack to the Isles.

[A cromack *is a walking stick; the* Cuillins *are a mountain range on the Isle of Skye; a* loch *is a lake.*]

Walking Song

As suits a Swiss song, this tune has a fine yodel in it. A yodel is a refrain of meaningless syllables sung in a falsetto voice, popular among the mountain folk of the Swiss and Tyrol mountains.

JAUNTILY

Swiss traditional

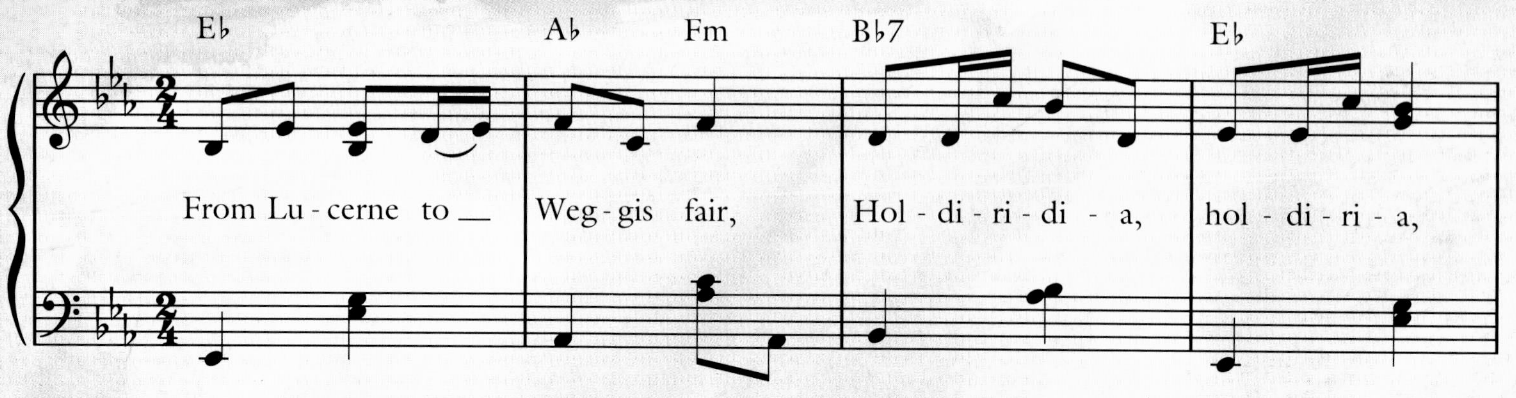

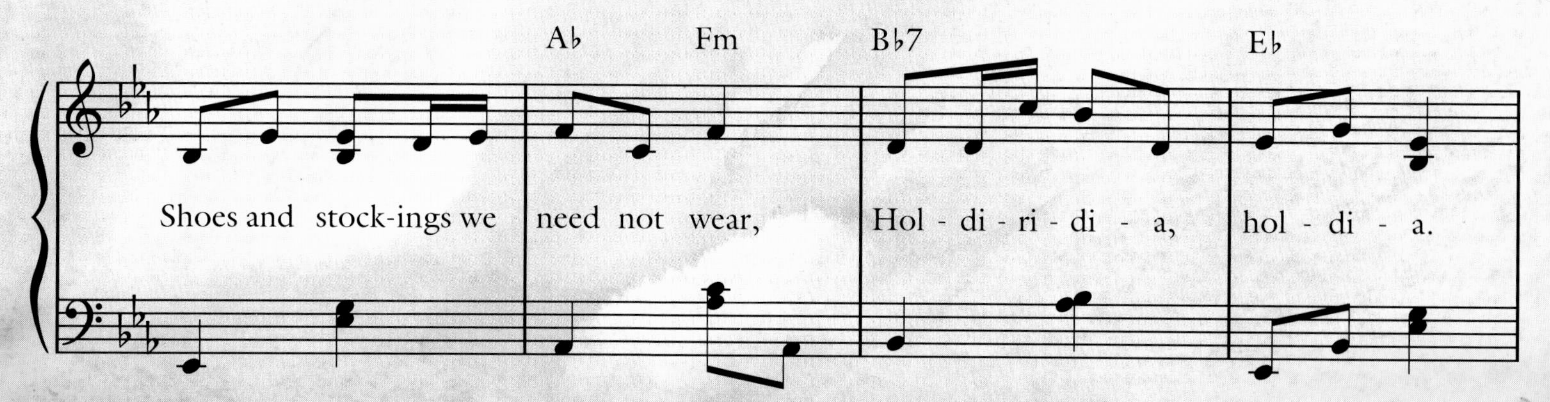

A♭ E♭ B♭7 E♭
Hol - di - ri - di - a, hol - di - ri - di - a, hol - di - ri - a.
A♭ E♭ B♭7 E♭
Hol - di - ri - di - a, hol - di - ri - di - a, hol - di - a.

The Foot Traveler

This energetic song about an equally energetic walker comes from Germany.

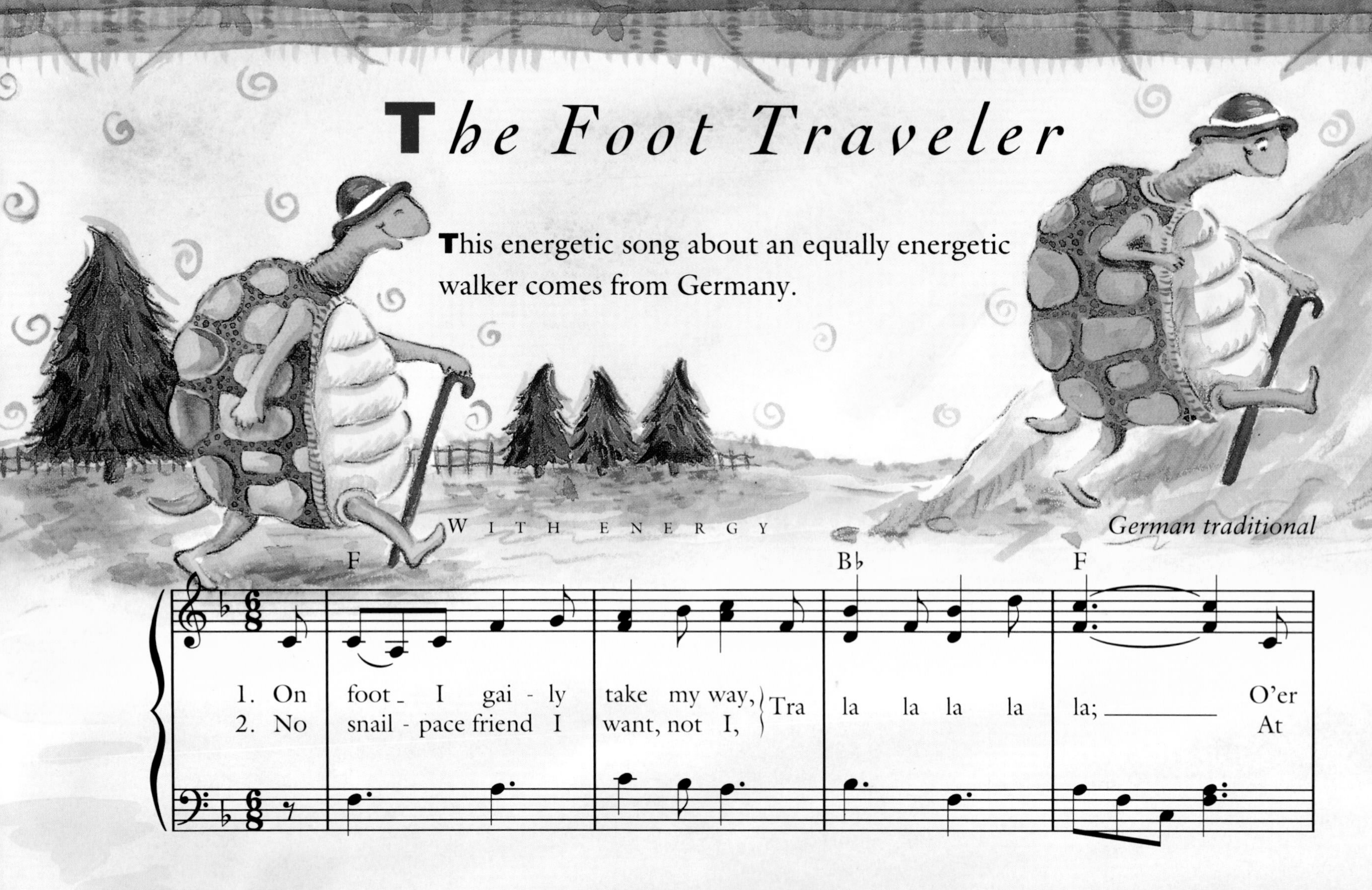

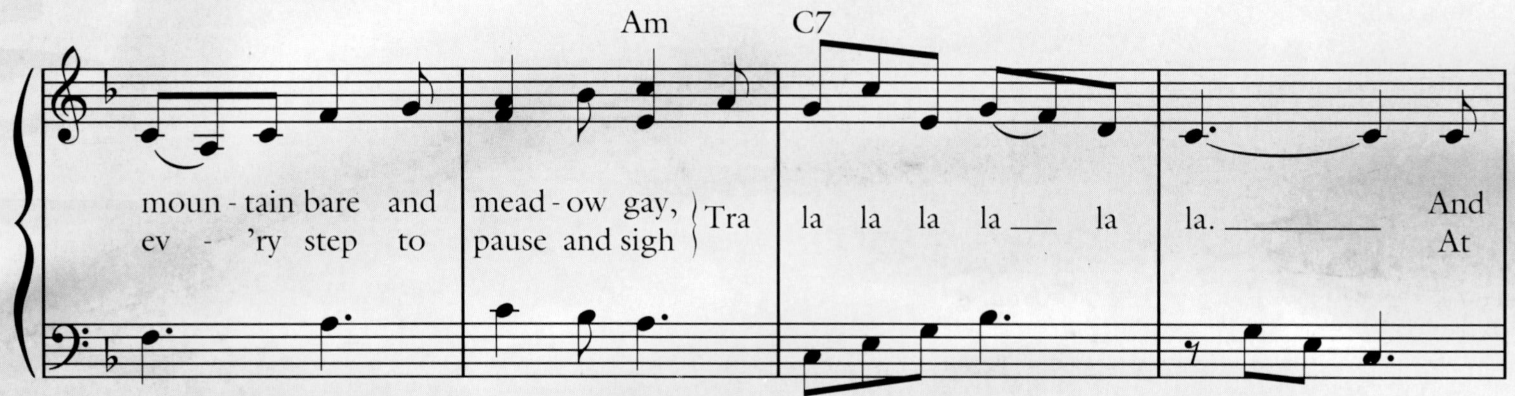

Gm C Gm C7
he who is not of my mind, An - oth - er trav' - ling mate must find, He
ev - 'ry step to sigh and groan, And o - ver o - thers' sins to moan, I'd

F B♭ F C7 F
can - not walk with me, he can - not walk_ with me.
rath - er walk a - lone, I'd rath - er walk_ a - lone.
Tra la la
More

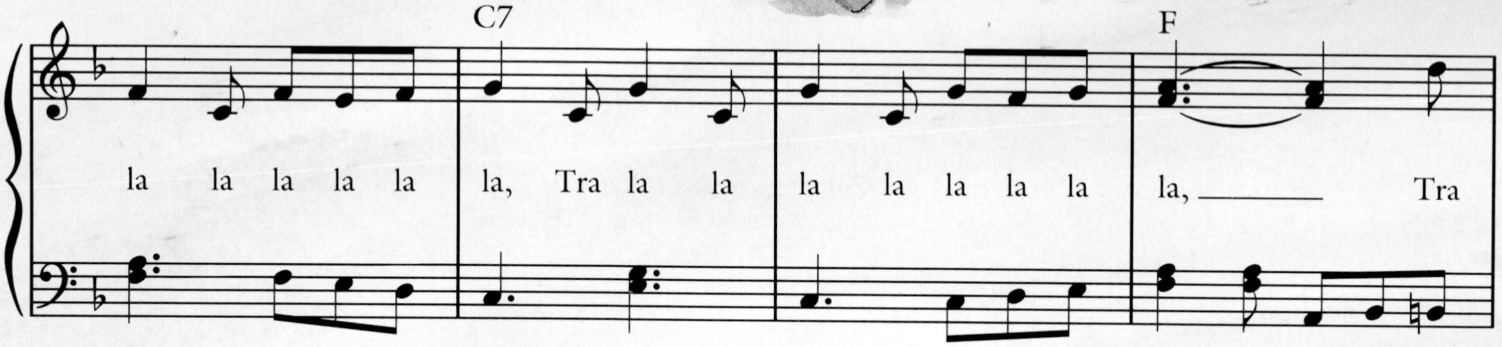

C7
F
la la la la la
la, Tra la la
la la la la la
la, ——— Tra

C7
F
C7
F
la, ——— Tra
la, ——— Tra
la la la la la
la. ———

Summer Breeze

Based on an old folk rhyme about gardens, the verse was set to music by the British composer John Langland.

GENTLY

John Langland

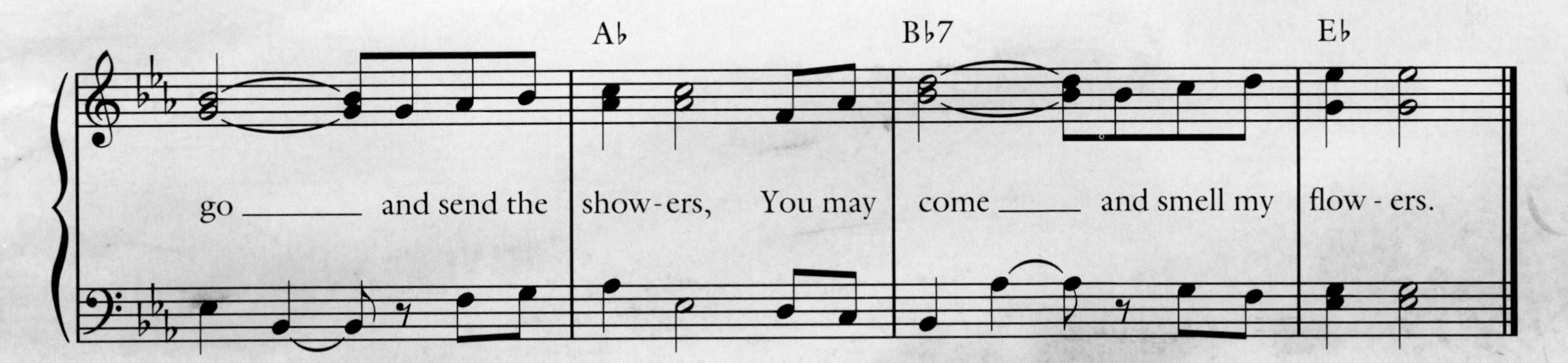

Wild Mountain Thyme

Popular in Ireland and Scotland, this song has become a staple of the folk-singing world.

WITH FEELING

Scottish / Irish traditional

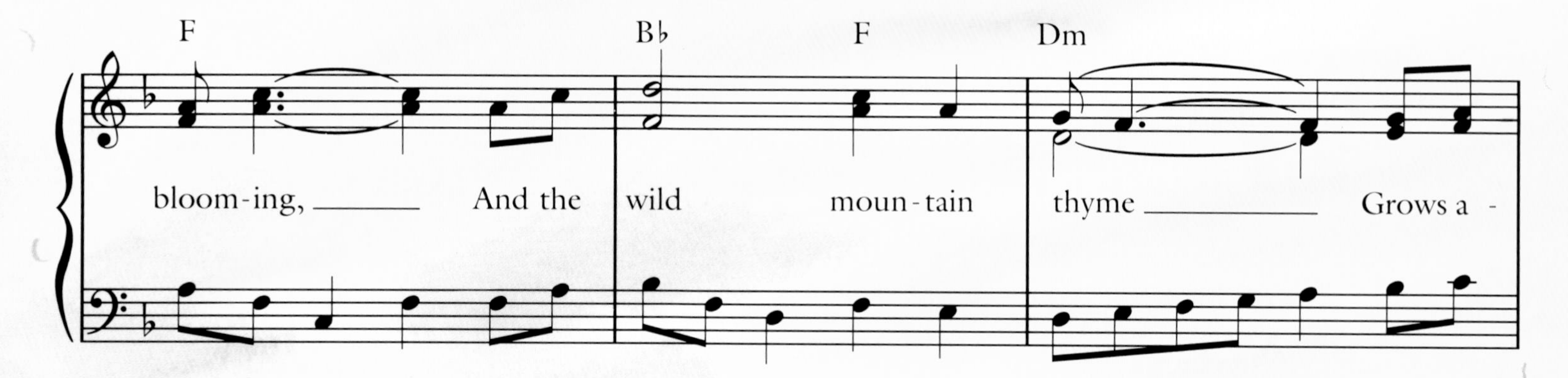

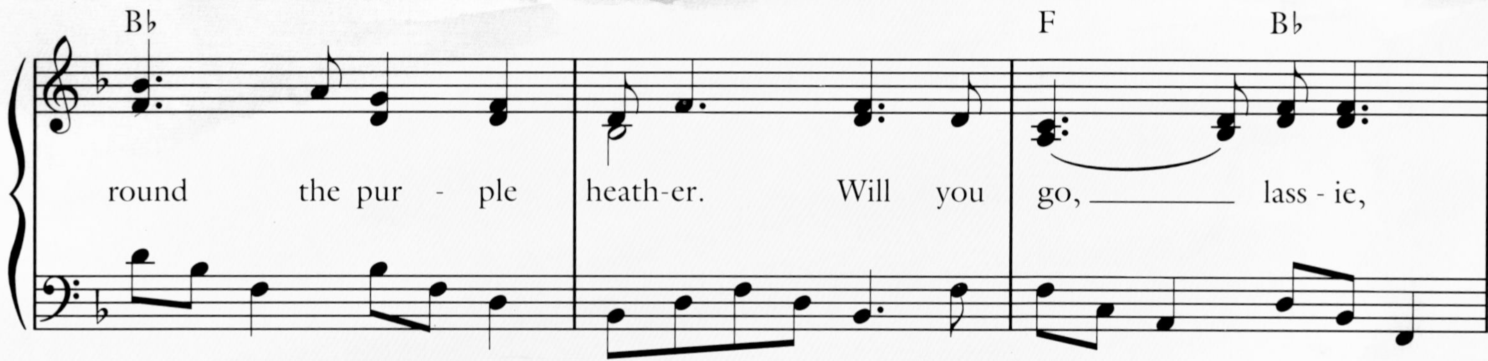

B♭
F
B♭
round the pur - ple heath-er. Will you go, lass - ie,

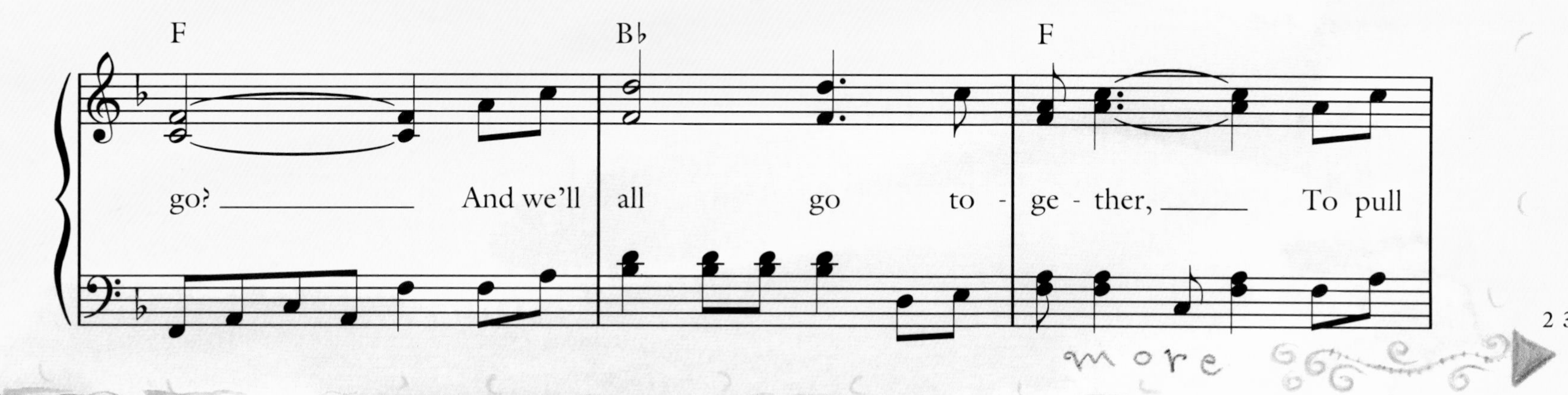

F
B♭
F
go? And we'll all go to - ge - ther, To pull
more

2. I will build my love a tower
By yon clear crystal fountain,
And on it I will pile
All the flowers of the mountain.
Will you go, lassie, go?

And we'll all . . . etc.

3. If my true love should me leave
I shall surely find another
To pull wild mountain thyme
All around the purple heather.
Will you go, lassie, go?

And we'll all . . . etc.

It's a Rosebud in June
A very traditional English tune, this sheepshearing song has been collected all over the British Isles.
SWEETLY
English traditional
Em
Bm
C
D
E
1. It's a rose-bud in June and violets in full bloom, And the
2. O when we have sheared all our jol-ly, jol-ly sheep, What
Em
G
A
E
small birds singing love songs on ev'ry spray.
joy can be greater than to talk of their in-crease?
We'll
more

G Em Bm C D Em G A C
pipe and we'll sing,_ love, we'll_ dance in a ring,_ love, When each
Em D A G A C D E C
lad takes his lass all ___ on the green_ grass, And it's
G Em Bm C D E
all ___ to plough_ Where the fat ox - en

Am G D Em Bm C D G A Em
graze low, And the lads and the lass - es to sheep-shear-ing go.

Shuckin' of the Corn

A popular American traditional song, this tune often was sung at corn-shucking or corn-husking parties in the late summer. Hidden among the corn would be one red ear, and whoever found it could kiss anyone of his, or her, choice.

WITH GOOD HUMOR

American traditional

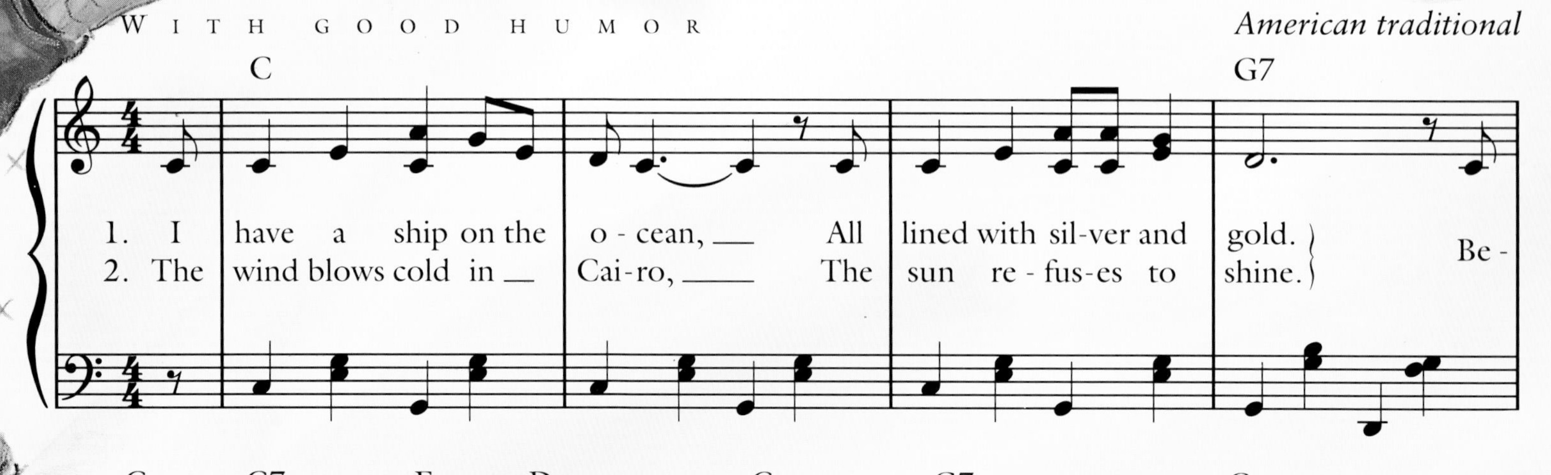

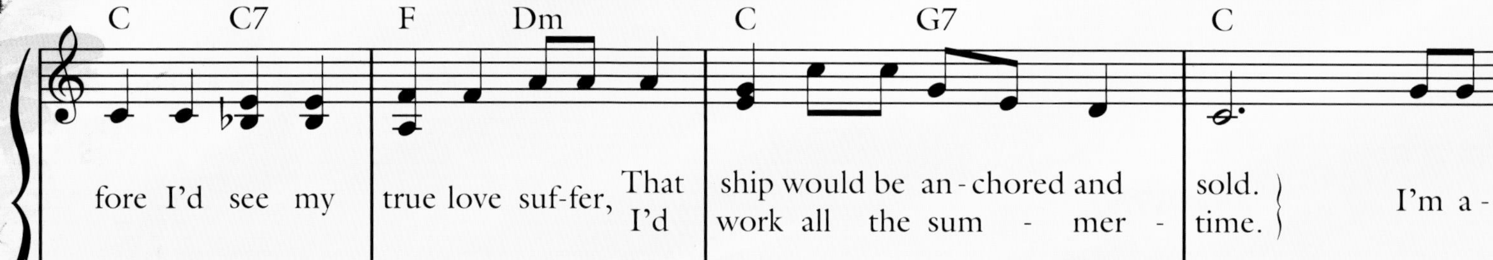

G7
go-in' to the shuck-in' of the
corn,
I'm a -
go-in' to the shuck-in' of the
corn,
A -
C
C7
F
Dm
C
G7
C
shuck-in' of the corn and a
blow-in' of the horn, I'm a -
go-in' to the shuck-in' of the
corn.

Summer's End

Based on a winter poem ("Snow, snow, shiver and blow. . .") first published in the children's magazine *Cricket* and later expanded, this song bemoans summer's end.

Am
C/G bass
F
D7/F# bass
Am
Ber - ry brown, ver - y brown,
We're quite a sight.
Dry is the lawn
Then
Wink-ing out, blink - ing out
Fire - fly light.
Off a - gain on
D
G7
1.
C
G
G7
sum - mer is gone.
2.
C
G
G7
C

A Note from the Author

I learned a great many songs at summer camp, like "Canoe Round" and the boisterous "Road to the Isles," which we always sang with rather more gusto than talent. It is amazing what fresh air, summer sun, and an absence of parents can do for a song.

My own children learned these songs from me on our camping holidays, which took us from the coast of Maine to the West Virginia hills, across the Continental Divide to California's Donner Pass. It is even more amazing how history and moonlight can affect a song.

When it came time to create this book, Adam and I remembered many of those songs, learned some new ones—and made up even more. We hope you will find out what transforms the songs for you—whether it is classroom participation, a quiet tent, or the loud companionship at a campfire where flames and music keep away the dark.

—Jane Yolen